STRAW INTO GOLD

A RUMPELSTILTSKIN FAERIE TALE RETELLING

CAROL BETH ANDERSON

Straw into Gold: A Rumpelstiltskin Faerie Tale Retelling by Carol Beth Anderson

Published by
Eliana Press
P.O. Box 2452
Cedar Park, TX 78630

Originally published in *Villainous: An Anthology of Fairytale Retellings*

www.carolbethanderson.com

Front Cover Design:
Rebecca F. Kenney

Paperback ISBN: 978-1-949384-20-8

y feet are bare, and I'm wearing a tiny dress made of spider silk, flowers, and ferns. In short, I'm scandalous.

Or I would be, could anyone see me.

Fae magic has its perks, like the ability to wander invisibly through a throne room. I let my fingers lightly brush the silks and furs of snooty courtiers, laughing when they flinch.

My gaze locks on the faces of the few desperate commoners lucky enough to get an audience with the king. I'm looking for some recognizable trait—that slender nose that ran in Father's family; or the brown hair, tinged with copper, that Mother passed on to me. But no one looks familiar. I don't know why I keep hoping I'll find someone who's heard of me. Someone who knows my name.

The herald's voice bounces off the marble floors and arched ceilings. "Presenting Mister Amos Miller!"

I glance at two men, both bowing low before the king. One is shorter and middle aged, with a bit of a paunch and a head full of dark auburn hair. My eyes are moving from him to his companion when the king bids them both rise, and … good heavens, the second man, who must be in his early twenties, is handsome enough to nearly make me feel like a human again. I approach him on quiet feet to get a better look.

He's as tall as I am—an impressive feat not one in ten men can claim. His hair is thick, wavy, and brighter than his father's—the shade of autumn leaves kissed by the sun. His fair skin is freckled—not the scattering of distinct brown dots my own face bears, but a crowding of tawny spots, big and little, covering every square inch of his face, neck, and, from what I can see between the loose lacing of his shirt, his chest.

His shirt is nothing special; every peasant in the country has one just like it. On him, however, it's eye catching, stretching across broad shoulders that don't shy away from hard work. I'll give the sleeves credit; they do their best to hide his strength, but they fail miserably in their quest.

My gaze continues to wander, to his eyes—blue like mine, but paler. And his full lips. And his broad hands, nearly as freckled as his face. I haven't seen a human this intriguingly good-looking in the last five years … or two hundred, depending how you count.

All at once, I realize I've spent half a minute ogling this young man, paying no attention as the king talks with the older man. I'll never be allowed to leave home again if I don't make the most of my time away. And making the most of it does not include drooling over a miller's son. I shift my attention to what King Edwin is saying.

" … see no reason why we should allow you to continue leasing the mill, when a man with three strapping young sons wishes to increase its output significantly!"

"Your Majesty, thank you for granting us an audience," the miller says, and that single, slurred sentence informs me of one horrifying fact: this man is drunk. He probably wanted to fortify his courage before meeting the king, but he went too far. His son's lips turn white as he presses them together. The miller continues, "My son is worth three— nay, a dozen! a hundred!—other sons. He's the hardest worker you ever met. And it's not just the mill! His talents are splendless … ah, they're endlessed. Splendissly endlessed, Your Majesty. He cooks like a chef and even spins the finest wool—"

The king's booming laughter interrupts the miller. "He cooks and spins wool? Like a woman?"

I take note of the young man's cheeks, which are a quite lovely shade of pink now.

"Oh, Your Majesty, no, his mother … she died nigh on eight—seven—ah, nine years ago, and she was the best spinner in the land. She taught him all she knew!"

"As lovely as that is"—the king lets out a dramatic sigh —"I fail to see how your son's odd hobbies affect your ability to run a mill that I own." He turns to the secretary sitting at a little desk to his left. "When the lease comes up for renewal, transfer it to the family who appealed to me last week."

"Your Majesty!" The miller's exclamation is loud enough to silence the room. The king glowers. That should send the man scurrying away, but liquor has drowned his reason. He places a shaking hand on his son's back. "You don't want to lose the service of me and my son, oh no, you don't!"

I start to turn away. I'm here to trick someone out of their riches, and this family is clearly on the way down, not up. But the man's next slurred statement causes me to halt.

"In fact, my son is so talented, he can spin straw into gold!"

Everyone in the room gasps—all except the king,

whose lips form a cruel smirk. Every eye is on him as he beckons two guards and whispers to them.

Seconds later, the guards are leading the miller and his son into a torchlit corridor. I follow close behind. The miller begins to blubber, his sobs echoing on the stone walls. His son tries to yank his arm away from the guard, but a cuff to the ear and a muttered threat bring him in line. At the end of the corridor, the guards pull their captives in opposite directions.

"Where are you taking my father?" the young man demands in a deep voice I could happily listen to for hours.

"To the dungeon."

"And me?"

His guard laughs. "You're gonna spin straw into gold."

That settles it, I'm following the young man, not his soon-to-be-imprisoned father. As we walk through dim corridors, I recall the conversation that brought me here.

I was at home, the forest clearing where I've lived with Him for the last five years. *Him*—my master, the Fae whose name I don't know.

"We're running short on money," He said. "We'll need to find more."

Find meant *steal*. We'd gone on many such quests, both of us sneaking invisibly through human communities, pilfering coins or valuables. One good day of thievery could provide enough money to buy food for weeks or months.

I approached Him, standing so close that I had to lift my chin to look in his eyes. "I'd like to go alone this time. I think I'm ready." My lips curved with the smile he loves— soft and sweet, with a hint of promise.

His gaze flicked across my features, and I held my breath until he smiled and said, "Go, but return as soon as you can. You'll have invisibility and any other magic you'll need, within reason."

I nearly kissed him.

Nearly.

Not knowing if I'd ever get another chance at such freedom, I went straight to the castle. What better place to encounter wealthy people … and get a taste of royal luxury?

I didn't, of course, anticipate meeting a man who could spin straw into gold. His father was probably lying, but what if he wasn't? If I return to the clearing with news of a human wielding such magic, He'll trust me as He never has. He may even tell me His name.

The guard stops at a heavy, wooden door. He pulls out a key, opens the door, and pushes the young man inside. I slip in behind him.

"A servant will be back with the straw," the guard says, laughter in his voice. "You'll have 'til morning to spin it into gold."

The room is faintly lit by a single, small window near the ceiling. It's enough light for me to see the young man's throat lurch as he swallows hard. "And if I don't?"

"We'll behead you." The guard gives him a wicked grin, then pulls the door shut and locks it.

"Damn it!" the man before me shouts, and swearing has never been so attractive.

He turns in a slow circle. I do the same. The room contains two items: a stool and a small, wooden spinning wheel. He crosses to the spinning wheel, then examines it and touches—no, more like *caresses*—it, running his fingers along the long, narrow quill spindle and the rim and spokes of the wheel. He sits and works the pedal, sending the wheel spinning smoothly. I doubt this man can spin straw into gold, but he clearly knows how to use this tool.

He stands and paces. I lean against the wall, eyeing his long legs and broad chest. If the man I was once intended to marry had looked like this, I'd never have run off.

Perhaps a half hour passes before a key rattles in the lock. The miller's son runs up to the door, fist clenched and drawn back, ready to punch whoever comes in.

Unfortunately, it's not a person who enters first—it's the front wheel of a wheelbarrow, full of straw, pushed by a male servant. The miller's son steps back, lowering his fist. He sighs when the guard, bearing a naked sword, follows the servant into the room.

The servant unloads the straw onto the floor as another man brings in several torches, lighting them and mounting them in sconces on the walls.

"Happy spinning!" the guard says as they all exit.

The miller's son kneels at the straw, muttering something. More curses? A prayer? He picks up a few pieces of straw, plops down on the stool, and starts to work.

I'm so enamored by his focus—squinty eyes, pursed lips, confident hands—that it takes an embarrassingly long time for me to realize he's failing at his task. He can't even get the straw to stay on the narrow quill spindle, much less convince it to transmute itself into gold.

On silent feet, I step toward him. A foot away from the spinning wheel, I stop, suddenly hesitant. Fashions have changed since I last lived among humans, but basic rules of female modesty haven't. In the world beyond this room, skirts extend to the floor. Feet and ankles are covered in boots. Sleeves are never shorter than elbow length, and necklines live up to their name, extending at least to the base of the neck.

And I'm about to approach a man and introduce myself with three-quarters of my legs showing and every bit of my arms. Even my shoulders are nearly bare, my straps thin as the piece of straw in the man's hand; and my neckline dips a full three inches below my collarbones. It's terribly unseemly.

And maybe a little thrilling.

But I'm not here to seduce or to shock. I'm here to get funds for food, so perhaps He will trust me enough to let me take more solitary excursions. I've given up hope of finding true freedom—even now I can feel the mystical cord tying me to Him. However, journeys like this might keep me sane in the endless years of immortality.

It's time to get down to business. "Hello," I say softly as I fade into view.

He stands so quickly, his stool topples. "Damn it!" That must be as severe as his curses get, because I can't imagine he's ever been as astounded as he is right now. His eyes find the door, beyond which a guard is surely standing. He lowers his voice. "Where did you come from?"

"I've been here. You simply couldn't see me."

He draws back. "You're Fae."

"No, I'm human." Sort of.

He's recovered enough to really look at me. His eyes flick down, then up, not lingering anywhere but on my face. "Aren't you cold?"

The question brings tears to my eyes, though I can't imagine why. I blink before they can spill over. "I don't get cold," I say. "I'm human, but I've been given some Fae gifts. I don't ever feel cold or hot. I don't age." I point to my face. "Even my freckles stay the same, no matter how much time I spend in the sun." I have no idea why I'm telling him all this, but I can't seem to stop. "The flowers and ferns on my dress don't wilt or rot. And I can spin that straw into gold."

As I speak, his eyes widen. He opens and closes his

mouth a couple of times before finally speaking. "You can spin straw into gold?"

If I were just a woman, I'd do this as an act of kind-ness, no payment required, though I'd hope for a smile in return. Then again, if I were just a woman, I couldn't help him a bit. I'm more than a woman and also less than one, and I need something more practical than a smile. "I'll do it for that silver chain around your neck." I let my eyes drop for a moment to the glimmer of silver resting against that beautiful, sharp corner where his neck meets his shoulder.

His brows draw together. "If you can make gold, why do you need my silver?" He's still speaking quietly, but there's an edge to his voice now, a challenge.

"Fae-made gold will turn back to straw if I have it in my hands for longer than a few moments. Don't worry—it won't change for you or the king."

His eyes lock with mine for several seconds before he grasps the chain with his long, beautiful fingers and lifts it over his head. When he pulls it off, I see a silver ring on it. "The chain only," he says firmly. "The ring was my mother's."

I should demand both. He—in the pragmatic way of the Fae—would tell me not to settle for only the chain. But I can't take this man's mother's ring. "We have a deal," I say.

He puts the ring on his smallest finger. It lodges halfway down the digit. Holding out the chain, he seems to realize I have no pockets. So he places the necklace over my head, trapping my long hair between the silver and my neck. He grasps my hair, then catches himself. "May I?"

The sweetness of the question nearly breaks my resolve. This man and his father will probably still lose their mill, and I'm taking a silver chain from him that could feed them for weeks. But I have no choice. If I go home empty-handed, He may never trust me enough to release me again.

I realize I haven't answered his question. "Yes, of course." I keep my voice hard and practical, as if I'm used to being touched by men I just met.

He pulls my hair free, his fingers brushing against my neck. I shiver.

His smile brightens the room. "I thought you couldn't feel cold."

I ignore the question and turn away. A moment later, I'm on the stool. "Show me how this thing works."

Getting the straw to spiral onto the quill spindle is terribly difficult, and my fingers brush against his far too many times in the process. His shirt, too, slides across my skin, and it's softer than any homespun fabric I've ever felt. I don't need to ask if he spun the thread; I know he did.

At last, a piece of yellow straw is spiraled around the slim rod of metal, and my bare foot is pumping the pedal beneath. Magic flows from my chest to my arms to my hands … and as the straw I hold twists, it turns to thin, flexible, golden thread. Heart pounding, I spin the entire strand of straw and hold out a hand for another piece, looking up as I do so.

Firelight flickers off the wide, blue eyes of the miller's son. He grins, bigger than before, and instead of handing me more straw, he takes my hand and shakes it. "Well done. I'm Cole."

My heart drops a bit. I can't tell him my name. "I … I need more straw." I pull my hand free.

His smile disappears. "Of course."

We get in a rhythm, me spinning, him handing me pieces of straw. As my fingers draw out the straw, turning it to gold, and my foot works the pedal, I let my mind wander back to the day I lost my name.

I'd met Him a week before, on a walk through the forest. He hadn't tried to hide His Fae nature, and that made me trust Him. He claimed He was different, that He wouldn't abduct me as other Fae might, that He'd never steal my virtue, that He'd in fact been rejected by his own people for His strange sense of ethics. After a week of clandestine meetings, I believed Him.

I was desperate to escape the marriage my parents had planned for me. Roland, the baker's son, was kind enough, but he was as bland as bread baked without salt. I couldn't imagine living the next half century of my life with him. A gorgeous, thoughtful Fae male who praised my beauty and wit seemed the perfect escape.

When He asked me to run away with Him, I agreed.

"First," He said, "please give me your name."

I froze. I didn't know much about the Fae, but like everyone else, I knew my name would give Him control over me.

When I refused, He explained it differently. "I can only give you my heart—and my magic—if you give me your name. It will create a beautiful bond between us. But it's your choice. Whatever you decide, I will one day give you my name, thus giving you control over me."

His assurances—and His kisses, which were unlike any I'd gotten from the boys in the village—nearly convinced me. But I couldn't quite let go of my fear. "If I give you my name, then regret it," I said, "is there a way to break the bond between us?"

He pulled me into his arms and breathed, "Don't you know?"

"Know what?"

"If anyone else—human or Fae—speaks your name to you again, the bond will break."

That promise convinced me. I gave him my name—a long, dreadful thing. I expected him to roar with laughter like most people did. My father, a linguist of sorts, had mixed together bits of different languages into a cumbersome name that roughly translated to *beautiful river under the sun*. I wish he'd settled on Betty or Mary instead.

Rather than laughing, my Fae spoke my name as if it were a prayer. I sensed the bond it created between us, the magic and immortality it granted me. That night, we stepped past a ring of toadstools into a Faerie circle and emerged into the heartbreakingly beautiful realm of the Fae. On a bed of moss in a cavern lit by glowing crystals, I gave myself to him completely.

When I woke the next morning, regret had dug its claws into me. I turned to Him and said, "I didn't tell my family goodbye. I didn't break things off with Roland. Take me back so I may say farewell."

He blinked, then stood and said, "One moment." He left but soon returned, holding the most beautiful, gossamer dress, adorned with flowers and ferns. "I asked a Fae tailor to make this for you."

I dressed, delighting in the light, beautiful fabric. "Shall we go?"

"Pel …"

I smiled. It was the same nickname my youngest sister always used for me. "Yes?"

"I don't know what we'll find when we return."

"I've only been gone a night. They may be panicked, but they'll be happy to see me."

He didn't say another word, merely walked me back to my own world.

The forest felt different, though I couldn't pinpoint

why. We ran through it on bare feet, our energy seeming limitless.

When we emerged from the trees, everything had changed.

The village was three times the size it had been. People rode in covered, horse-drawn carts, lighter than the wagons I was used to. All the clothing looked strange. I recognized no one.

"Time can pass differently in the land of the Fae," was all He said.

Chest tight with dread, I ran into the village. Mothers covered their children's eyes, and both men and women gaped at my state of undress. Most people ignored my urgent questions, and when someone finally answered me, I ran back to the forest, weeping.

Nearly two hundred years had passed. Overnight.

I sat at the base of a tree, avoiding Him. When my tears were spent, I ran back to the village. I grabbed a kindly, elderly woman's arm. "Say my name," I begged. "It's—" But my mind went blank, my throat closed up, and my tongue became stiff.

I walked back to the forest, shoulders stooped, until I found Him. "Why didn't you tell me time might pass differently?"

"I had no way of knowing how much time would pass. And I didn't expect you to want to return."

"Why can't I remember my name?"

"It belongs to me now, not to you. Did we not speak of that?"

No, we certainly hadn't. "Take me to the village," I said. "Tell someone my name so they can speak it and break our bond."

"Oh, darling." He took my face in his hands, the green

of his eyes bright in the tree-dappled sunlight. "Why would I do that?"

That was five years ago. We've stayed in the land of humans since then. He knows that taking me back to the realm that stole my life—stole my family, stole my very *era*—would send me into such deep despair, I'd find it impossible to ever love him.

And that's his goal. To make me love him. I tell him it won't work. He smiles and asks to kiss me. I say no. He respects my answer. Is he better than other Fae? I'm sure he is. Yet He refuses to break our bond. And He's never given me His own name.

A tear drops from my cheek, landing on my thigh.

"Does this hurt your hands?" Cole asks. "We can take a break."

I lower my head, letting my hair fall over my face, sniffling softly. "I'm fine."

And I am, or at least my hands are. Fae magic makes them strong.

I work, refusing to let my mind wander again. I focus on the straw, twisting it into gold. I gaze at the growing spool of shimmering thread on the spindle. At some point, we slip it off and start another skein of priceless thread.

Cole's quiet voice breaks the silence. He tells me how frightened he was when his father made his rash promise to the king. His father, he explains, is drunk most of the time. Over the years, the man has begun living more and more in a fantasy world.

When Cole thanks me profusely for my help, his silver chain weighs heavy on my neck. At least I didn't take the ring.

"Tell me about your mother," I say.

He does, praising her in a way we only praise those

who've been gone long enough for us to forget their faults. I get the feeling she's the one who turned him into the good man he is—the man who continues her legacy of spinning and is doing all he can to save his father and their mill.

Cole goes on to tell stories of his cousins, his neighbors, his simple life. He's not one to build himself up, but I hear the truth behind his humble words. His community respects him. They depend on his generosity, and he comes through for them, even when he has little to give.

As he talks, I occasionally hear the ringing of distant church bells. I'm too enthralled by Cole's voice to pay attention to what hour it is. At last, the final piece of straw has been turned into gold. We have four thick skeins of glittering thread to present to the guard. It can be woven into fabrics or melted down and made into anything the king wishes.

I look up at the little window. "It's already dusk."

Cole's laugh is as soft as his voice has been over the preceding hours. "No, it's nearly dawn."

"You must be kidding!"

"I'm not." He's been on his knees for some time, and he stands and lifts his arms high, stretching.

I do the same. My body, sheltered by Fae magic, is not sore, but stretching still feels good. When my eyes find Cole, he quickly pulls his gaze from my legs, muttering, "Sorry."

"I'm sure you're not used to seeing women in Fae dress."

He gives me a bashful smile. "That's true." His smile fades. "Please tell me your name."

"I can't," I say, "but you can call me Pel." As always, my heart aches at the moniker. I miss my little sister. I miss my real name.

"Pel. Thank you."

I don't have time to respond. A key clatters in the lock. I disappear, and the door opens.

When the guard sees the skeins of golden thread, his jaw drops. He turns and leaves wordlessly. I follow him out.

"Goodbye," Cole calls. I know he's not talking to the guard.

I have the silver chain. I should go back to my forest clearing, but something keeps me in the guard's shadow, my bare feet following him silently through the corridors.

I stay with him when he brings the gold to the king, though I don't manage to squeeze through the doorway. When he returns to the hallway, I follow him back to the locked room with the spinning wheel and the red-haired man. Inside, the guard explains that in an hour, a larger load of straw will be delivered, and Cole must spin it all into gold by tomorrow morning, or he'll lose his head.

My heart pounding, I leave with the guard.

As the door closes, I hear Cole's two-word response, little more than a growl.

"Damn it."

It takes me an hour to run through the capital city, the spring-green hills, and the thick forest. I estimate it's twenty miles to my home, and I'm not the least bit winded when I arrive. I'm also not sleepy. Fae magic eliminates the need for nightly rest, though we often sleep out of boredom. I can't remember when I last felt legitimately tired. Sometimes I miss it, just as I miss being cold or hot.

I step into the clearing and find Him reclining by a low fire. He leaps to his feet and approaches me.

Even after five years, I'm still shocked by how handsome He is. More than that, He's *beautiful* in the ethereal manner of the Fae. His eyes are bright green, His perfectly shaped lips perpetually begging to be kissed. Glossy, pale blond hair streams down His back, nearly to his waist. Even His ears are stunning, tapering to sharp points.

Then there's His skin and His form. He looks like He was carved from a block of gold by a master artist who loved sharp, artistic lines. His muscles, jaw, nose, cheekbones—all are beautifully defined, shimmering in the sun.

He was dressed in nothing but pants when I first met Him, and I've since learned that's His normal state. Looking at Him now, I remember why I first gave myself to Him. Feeling the temptation to do so again, I try to remember my name. The grief of its loss helps me shield myself from His charms.

He's smiling as he strides to me and takes my hands, His eyes swirling with as much longing as ever. His gaze flicks to my neck, and His smile widens as He releases my hands and takes hold of the chain. He doesn't seek permission for His golden fingers to glide along my skin. He doesn't ask if he can move my hair to pull the chain off.

"Well done, Pel," he says. "Tell me about it."

"It'll have to be fast. I think I can get more if I go back."

We sit by the fire. He gives me dried berries and roasted nuts, and I tell my story. My descriptions of Cole are pragmatic—no mention of autumn-leaf hair or well-worked muscles—but He must hear something in my voice, because He crosses his arms, and His eyes narrow.

"I'll give you all the magic you need," He says, "but this boy must pay what you deserve. You cannot help him for free."

"He can't pay me what the gold is worth!"

"Base the price on the value of the magic you're expending, not of the resulting gold. The ring you mentioned—it's important to him. It will be enough. Between it and this chain, we'll be fed for weeks. Months, perhaps." His fingers find my shoulder and slide gently down my arm until He's holding my hand. "A kiss before you go?"

"No."

He rubs his thumb gently across my palm. "Soon, love."

I hate the desire His touch sparks in me. I fix another face in my mind—fair and freckled, topped with fiery hair. Then I stand and run toward the castle, not looking back.

I bang an invisible hand on the thick, wooden door, hoping the guard standing there will think his prisoner is knocking.

It works. When the guard checks on Cole, I enter the room, grimacing at the mounds of straw, twice as much as yesterday. As soon as the door is closed and locked again, I appear.

"Oh, thank heaven," Cole breathes. "Can you help me?"

Guarding myself against the way his words soften my heart, I whisper, "I'll need your ring."

His face falls. "Pel." When I don't respond, he yanks it off his finger and holds it out. His jaw is flexed, and I hate to say it, but he may be even more gorgeous like this, flush with silent fury.

I take the ring and fit it on my middle finger. "He told me I had to …" I begin. But why am I explaining? This is a business transaction. Even if my Fae master hadn't established this new rule about being paid what my magic is worth, I'd ask for the ring. Not because I'm afraid of going hungry, but because time away from Him is freedom, and I'll do whatever I must to keep earning these outings.

But my few words were enough to catch Cole's attention. His muscles loosen, and concern fills his eyes. "Who told you … who is *He*?"

I shake my head. "We need to get started. I don't know if I can spin all this by tomorrow morning. Did you get any rest?"

"Not much."

"Take a nap. When you're done, you can help me."

He must be exhausted, because he doesn't argue. I begin spinning, and I'm on my second skein of golden thread when he wakes, hair mussed and eyes bleary. He takes on his role again, handing me one piece of straw at a time.

I'd promised myself that we wouldn't converse today like we did yesterday, but Cole clearly made no such resolution. In his quiet, warm voice, he tells me lighthearted stories of life at the mill and of the spinning he does at night.

"You know," I say as my foot pumps the wheel's pedal and my magic twists the straw into gold, "you can't do everything."

"Why not?"

His question sounds completely honest, and I laugh. "Nobody can, Cole."

"Says the woman who's spinning straw into gold."

I finish the strand of straw I'm working on and remove my foot from the pedal, looking up at him. "For five years, I've done magical feats you can't imagine. But I'm more aware than ever of my limitations." I take the straw he's holding out, loop it onto the end of the golden thread, and continue spinning.

He's silent for so long, the whirl of the wheel sends me

into a near-trance. At last, he speaks. "Are you enslaved to a Fae man?"

My foot comes down too hard on the pedal, and the straw lurches from my hand. I stop the wheel and retrieve the end of the straw, my fingers trembling.

"You have Fae magic," Cole says, "and you mentioned a *He* who told you to take my ring. He's controlling you, isn't He?"

Forcing my hands and foot to return to their rhythmic task, I keep my voice light. "Who wouldn't give up a little freedom in exchange for immortality?"

"That's probably true. But I imagine more than a few people would regret that choice." As always, his voice is low, so the guard won't hear. However, there's a new gentleness in it now, a serrated kindness that rips into my heart.

I don't answer, just continue my task. After some time, he says, "What was your childhood like?"

I suspect he'd rather ask about my current life, but he's respecting my clear desire for privacy. While my body can't sense heat anymore, my soul can, and it fills with warm gratitude. I open my lips and let words pour out—tales of my older siblings who married young and showed me how hard life was, of my younger siblings who kept me laughing.

I speak of the things I loved about childhood. Swimming in a creek behind the house. Burning my tongue on freshly baked apple rolls. I tell him of the book of Faerie stories my father used to let me read, of how I'd give my left leg to have it in my hands again. He asks if it was accurate, and I just laugh. "If only," I say, before shifting to another topic.

As my tongue loosens, my hands and foot do the same, moving faster than ever. Hours pass, full of stiff straw and soft gold, of easy words and laughter. I've found such an efficient rhythm that I finish spinning with time to spare. The sky outside the window has just begun to lighten to gray. I pull the eighth skein of golden thread from the quill spindle and set it on the floor.

We both stretch, as we did yesterday. Then he stands directly in front of me. Despite my height, I feel small before him, with his shoulders extending far beyond mine and his muscular arms again begging to be freed from the confines of his sleeves.

"What can I do for you, Pel?" he asks.

Oh heavens, I love the question, and I hate it. "I told you, Cole. You can't do everything. You certainly can't save me."

The torches that haven't yet fizzled out illuminate his helpless eyes. He extends his arms, and I know I shouldn't, but I fall into them. I wrap my arms around his waist and lay my head on his shoulder. I'd assume his emotions were as immovable as his body if I couldn't feel his heart pounding rapidly, attempting to outpace my own.

He guides me to the floor, where I curl on his lap, and we sit without speaking until the key jiggles in the lock. I fade from view and slip off his lap so he can stand.

Only he doesn't stand, he bends at the waist and lowers his forehead to the floor. Because this time, the guard isn't alone.

"Stand up, boy," King Edwin says.

As Cole obeys, I tiptoe right up to the king. His gaze shines with delight and greed as he takes in the eight fat skeins of golden thread. "Come with me," he commands.

I, of course, follow. We walk halfway down the corridor, stopping at a door identical to the other one. A guard opens it, revealing a room much larger than the first, with three narrow windows instead of one. Mounds of straw cover the floor, at least five times what I spun yesterday. The spinning wheel is larger, made of metal instead of wood.

Standing before it is a woman who's perhaps eighteen or twenty—the most beautiful woman I've ever seen. She's a couple of inches shorter than me, with long, black hair that falls down her back in gentle waves. Her eyes—good heavens, I could get swept in by their full lashes and lost in their mahogany depths. Her light brown skin is perfectly smooth, her lips full and red, her bone structure the type I thought only sculptors could create. She's dressed in an embroidered gown that covers her completely yet does nothing to hide her lush figure. I've often been called beautiful, but standing before this woman, I feel like nothing, a lanky waif who belongs anywhere but at a castle.

I pull my gaze away. Cole is staring at her like he could devour her whole. Come to think of it, he's probably genuinely hungry; I doubt he's eaten in over two days. But seeing his gaping mouth and wide eyes, I'm having a hard time pitying him.

"This," King Edwin says, "is my daughter, Lisbeth. Spin the straw in this room into gold by tomorrow at dawn, and she will be your bride. If you fail, you'll lose your head."

The miller's son doesn't curse this time, just nods. Everyone leaves the room, including Lisbeth, who gives Cole a sultry smile on the way out.

The key turns in the lock, and I appear. "Time to focus, Cole," I say, and though my voice is quiet, it's got an edge to it I didn't expect.

He snaps out of his haze. His blue eyes meet mine. "I don't have anything else to give you."

I pause. I can't do this for free. And we don't have time

to bargain. "When you're a prince," I say, "give me a trunk full of treasures."

"Done."

"Promise me."

"I swear it."

I feel the rush of magic surging through my body. "No time for a nap today. Let's get started."

We hardly speak. There's too much to do. The metal spinning wheel is crafted with precision and oiled so that it spins incredibly smoothly. I work faster than ever, but there's so much straw. Too much.

It grows dark. I keep working. In the distance, I hear the peal of twelve bells. Then one. Two. Before I know it, it's four in the morning. Half the straw remains.

"Damn it," Cole and I murmur in unison. We share a smile, despite the hopelessness of our task.

I take my foot off the pedal and turn to the man who's kneeling next to me, holding up a piece of straw. "I need more magic," I say.

"Do you have to go back to Him?"

"No, He said I'd have all I need. But you have to pay, Cole."

"I'll promise you anything."

Completing this task will require more power than any I've ever accessed. I'll need deep Fae magic, the type that's stored in the trees and lilies and animals. The magic of life itself.

Cole's life would pay for it. The truth comes to me in a whisper, and for a moment, I don't believe it. I can't protect him from the executioner's blade by killing him.

Not his death, the whisper says. *His life.*

And I understand. These payments aren't going to me. They're going to my Fae master. He's the one who received the chain; He's the one I'll give the ring to. He wouldn't value Cole's death, but He'd value Cole's life.

Cole's *name*.

No. I can't ask that of the man before me. I can't ask him to enslave himself the way I have. I wouldn't demand such a thing of an enemy, much less a man I've begun considering a friend.

But the alternative is his head. Slavery is better than death. Or is it?

"What are you thinking?" Cole asks. When I don't respond, he swallows, and his voice grows rough. "If I'm executed, my father will be alone. I can't do that to him. When I marry the princess, I'll have access to the riches of the kingdom. Not just gold and jewels—land and titles too. I don't have anything to offer you now, but in the future, I'll give you anything."

Three of his words—*in the future*—latch onto my imagination. Maybe Cole doesn't have to lose his freedom. Maybe we can pass along that curse to someone else.

The idea filling my mind is terrible. Cruel. But if I go home and tell Him I couldn't do what it takes, He'll know I was weak. He'll guess I've fallen for the miller's son. He won't let me leave again. The thought of being trapped with my beautiful Fae master, of never escaping for long enough to remember the part of me that's human … it's too much. I need this deal. So does Cole.

So I speak in a whisper that sears my throat. "You'll bring your first child to Him. To the Fae who owns me. You'll tell Him your child's name."

Cole's eyes widen. He pulls in a shaky breath. "You want me to enslave my child?"

I don't answer. I can't.

The battle in Cole's eyes is fierce and clear. He's

weighing his future child against his own life. Against the loss his father would experience if his only child is executed.

Cole's brows draw together, and an angry frown compresses his lips.

I hate the position I've put him in.

"Yes," he says. "For my father. Yes."

Regret and relief battle in my chest. Then an astonishing wave of magic obliterates them both. I nearly topple from my chair, but Cole's hand finds my back, stabilizing me.

I return my attention to my task, and I spin with the power of the Fae, of the Earth, of Cole's child's freedom. The man kneeling next to me can barely hand me straw fast enough. The metal wheel begins to glow orange, then white, the odor of hot iron filling the room. Only magic keeps it from melting into a puddle at my feet.

Just as dawn breaks, I pull the last of the golden thread from the wheel. I turn to Cole, who hasn't spoken since he made his promise. I don't expect him to ever meet my gaze again, but his eyes are waiting for me, mournful and desperate.

He takes the skein of thread from me and drops it carelessly on the floor, then takes my hands. "Is there anything I can do to save my child?" The words barely make it through his tight throat. "Please, Pel."

The very essence of my Fae magic has bound him to his promise. Perhaps there's a way to undo that, but I don't know how.

Unless …

What if the Fae magic that's flowed through me for five years—the magic binding Cole to his word—was gone?

I glance up through one of the windows. The sky is painted with streaks as golden as the thread at our feet and as pink as Cole's flushed cheeks. Someone will be here any second. "If you learn my name and speak it to me," I say, "I'll no longer have Fae powers. There will be no magic to bind you."

"And you'll be free too," Cole whispers.

I nod. This is cruel, this hope I'm establishing in his heart and in mine. No one on this Earth knows my name but the Fae who enslaves me. But if Cole heard Him say it . . .

"How can I learn your name?" Cole asks.

The door's lock rattles.

I fade into invisibility, then bring my lips to Cole's ear and whisper, "Remember, when I hold the gold, it turns back to straw." As I say it, I pull a long length of golden thread from the nearest skein. I break it off and gather it into my fist.

The door opens.

King Edwin enters. I step behind Cole, barely breathing, watching as the leader of our land picks up a fat skein of golden thread. "My boy," he says, clapping Cole on the shoulder, "you shall marry my daughter." A shrewd gleam enters his eye. "Every morning before breakfast, you'll spend an hour spinning straw into gold. We shall be the wealthiest nation in the world."

I see Cole's shoulders drop, but surely he knows he needn't worry. I'll return to help him every day. He'll pay me from the royal coffers. We can make this work. I reach out and place an invisible hand on Cole's back, a message to him: *It'll be fine.*

"Come in, dear," the king says, beckoning toward the dark doorway.

Lisbeth enters, and her wide smile makes her even more lovely. She approaches Cole, draws him into her arms, and kisses him. His arms encircle her. He kisses her back.

I slip through the open door, my lips pressed tightly together, tears blurring my vision.

Cole has clearly made peace with his fate, and who could blame him? He's holding a beautiful princess in his arms, and his father's mill will be safe. The only cost will be a bit of time each morning … and the enslavement of his child.

The idea I had before the king entered seems silly now. But the golden thread in my hand has already turned into a thick handful of coarse straw, so I follow through with my plan. I use three pieces of straw to make an arrow on the floor of the castle, then another, and another. Once I'm outside, I leave more arrows on the ground, one each time I turn.

It takes far longer than usual to make my way to the clearing. He's waiting for me, the morning sun setting His golden skin aglow.

When I hand him the ring, He smiles, and when I tell Him of the promise I elicited, He laughs and praises me. "Let's replenish our food stocks," he says.

We both fade from sight and run to the capital. Once there, he uses his magic to make himself look human and to cover us with the illusion of courtier finery. We return to visibility. After pawning the jewelry, we purchase food to last us a good, long while. Then He strolls with me through the city streets. We eat lunch at a fine restaurant. He purchases candies for me, and we hire a carriage to take us on a long ride through a beautiful park.

Something has changed between us. There's a delight in the way He treats me, a new kindness in the compliments He showers on me, a trust in His eyes I've never seen.

After a lovely day, we fade from visibility in the

shadows between two buildings. He removes the illusions He placed on us, and we run back to the forest.

I don't even realize I'm holding onto the possibility of seeing Cole again until my heart falls when we return to the clearing and find it empty. It's a silly thing to wish for; even if Cole found me here, the chances of him learning my name would be slim. My Fae master rarely uses it. But at least if he'd shown up, I could have told him how sorry I am, for the child he hasn't yet fathered. For the future I stole, as mine was stolen.

I push the pointless thoughts from my mind and focus on the present. In the middle of the clearing, He stands, using his magic to create a crackling fire. I approach it, and it's so lovely, I almost don't care that I can't feel its warmth.

We feast on food we purchased, and as the sun slips below the trees, He leans in, His eyes dancing with fire-light. "Dance with me, Pel."

A pause, filled only by the thump of my heart.

"Yes," I say.

He pulls me to my feet. With a snap of His fingers, music, magical and intricate, fills the clearing. My left hand lands on the smooth skin of His bare shoulder, and He takes my other hand in His.

He dances like He does everything else—with exquisite grace and charm. The muscles of His arms and chest ripple as He spins me, dips me, pulls me close. His eyes are full of green fire, and when they capture mine, I can't look away.

We dance until the sun sets and the crickets add their voices to the enchanted music. When the stars and the fire are the only sources of illumination, the music slows, then fades away. Our feet stop moving, but we're still holding each other, and it seems we're one with the grass beneath our bare feet and the stars overhead. I know the connection I feel to Him is an effect of our bond; but the magic of it makes it no less real.

Why am I still fighting this? I spent three days with the type of human I've always wanted, only to see him in the arms of another, a beautiful woman he can grow old alongside. Why did I ever give Cole a second thought, when in this clearing waited a Fae I can stay young alongside?

I refuse to lie to myself. I'll never believe the loss of my freedom was worth all I gained. I can't trust the one who captured my name but won't share His own. And I'll always wish I could cram a lifetime of passion into seventy years, instead of relaxing into the slow charm of immortality.

Yet this is my life now. Immeasurably long and magical. Bonded with Him. All that's left is to make the best of it.

I know He's not out of breath from our dancing, but the firelight reveals the quick rise and fall of His golden chest. He lightly traces my lips with his thumb. "Kiss me, Pel."

And tonight, I don't want to say no.

His mouth is as perfect as it was when I kissed Him five years ago, and while there's no love in this kiss, there is need and passion, and tonight, that's enough. My hands and lips beg Him to make me forget what I've lost and what I want. He grants my wish, holding me tightly in this moment, His arms as strong as the bond my name created between us.

His lips leave mine and find my neck, my jaw, and then He's speaking in my ear, breathing the words I always crave and so seldom hear: "My Rumpelstiltskin."

The name, spoken aloud, draws our bond tighter than ever. I bask in the echo of those syllables, even as they fade again from my memory. "Say it again," I beg, longing to know my name, if only for a moment.

His lips leave my ear, and He meets my gaze. This time, He speaks loudly, His musical voice full of confidence in how impossible it is for me to escape the power of our bond. "My Rumpelstiltskin."

I take His face in mine, meaning to kiss Him again. But another voice, one I've grown far too fond of over the last three days, makes me halt.

"Rumpelstiltskin."

There's no warning—the bond snaps. I jolt, sensing the break in a place beyond touch, beyond sound, beyond the world of humanity. Deep in my spirit, I know that the commitment I elicited from Cole has shattered too. His first child will belong to him.

All at once, I realize several things. I'm cold, my bare arms and legs erupting into gooseflesh. The magical fire isn't warm. And the arms holding me feel like a prison.

I'm about to pull away, but it's not necessary. He lets go of me and sprints, with the strength of a full-blooded Fae, to the source of the voice. In the time it takes me to draw a breath of cold air, He reaches Cole and tackles him to the ground.

"No!" I scream, running on cold, bare feet that are terribly, humanly slow. "Stop!" I cry as I reach them.

Barely illuminated by the firelight, He's strangling Cole, whose strength, earned through countless hours of manual labor, is no match for that of the Fae atop him.

I pull futilely at His arm. "Stop!"

"Why?" He asks, His voice frighteningly calm.

Words flow from my mouth, born of desperate instinct. "I'll tell you my name." Now that it's mine again, I know He's forgotten it. "I'll be yours. All of me." I'm crying now. "Please stop."

He releases his grip and holds up His hands. In the firelight, those long fingers look vicious in a way they never have before. He's still sitting atop Cole, who's hacking, trying to regain his breath. "Very well. Tell me your name again."

Tears wash over my cheeks. "First, promise me his child won't belong to you. I know the agreement is broken. Swear to me you won't demand the same from him again."

"I'll swear as you ask. But you must agree to forfeit your right to ever be freed."

"I agree. I'm yours. Forever."

"His child is his alone. I swear it." I see the diamond-hard desire in His eyes. "What is your name?"

I take a half second to glory in the chill wind on my skin, then say, "Rumpelstiltskin."

"*My* Rumpelstiltskin," He breathes.

The bond snaps back into place, forcing me to my knees. I don't know my name. I'm no longer cold.

He climbs off the miller's son and kneels by me, pulling me into His arms. I keep my promise. I allow Him to hold me, allow the bond to numb my doubts, my despair. "Go, Cole," I say. "Go to the castle. I'll help you spin every day. You can pay us with treasures."

"An excellent plan," my Fae master says.

"Go, Cole," I say again. "Marry the princess. Live your life."

The arms around me tighten as Cole stands and runs away.

I let Him pull me to my feet. I raise my face, and He kisses me. With my eyes closed, it's easy to imagine His hair is red, His skin fair and freckled. He's gentler than I expected, like He's savoring this moment, when I've finally committed my eternity to Him. I try to lose myself in the kiss. I try not to cry.

At last, He pulls his lips from mine and simply holds me close, His grip tight and sure. My eyes are wide open again, gazing over His shoulder as I fight not to let my tears overflow. He whispers words of adoration to me, telling me I'm beautiful, promising me never-ending happiness. I do my best to believe Him.

Movement catches my gaze, and I stop breathing. Behind the Fae who's holding me, Cole is creeping closer, a finger to his lips. He's approaching on bare feet—he learned something from me, I suppose—and pulling an object from his pocket. The quill spindle.

Cole jams its narrow end into the ear of the Fae holding me.

My master roars—a vulnerable, pained sound unlike anything I've ever heard. His arms loosen, and He falls to the ground, moaning, eyes rolling wildly.

And it hits me. This isn't the spindle from the wooden spinning wheel. It's from the metal wheel. Crafted from the only substance toxic to Fae—iron.

Cole twists the spindle in His ear. Dark, thick blood streams to the grass. "Let her go," Cole demands. "Release her from her bond."

The Fae who's enslaved me for five years can barely speak. "I … will not … bond her to you."

"I don't want to own her." There's a bubbling, quiet rage in Cole's response. "No one will ever own her again! Release her completely, you bastard."

As I wait for His response, I marvel that Cole knows more than one curse word.

"She's mine," the once-powerful Fae murmurs. "We have … an agreement."

Cole shoves the quill spindle deeper into His ear, and a terrified, pained moan emerges from that golden throat. "You can release her from the agreement any time you want," Cole says. "Do it, and we'll leave you alone."

I wait for Him to argue, but He doesn't. And somehow, I know the truth. All of it.

He knew centuries might pass when he brought me to the land of the Fae. He knew I didn't understand the realities of my enslavement. Being Fae, He cannot lie, but He hid the truth away, along with my freedom. He hid it behind clever evasions and sweet smiles and requests for kisses. I didn't need someone else to speak my name to free me. He could've broken our bond any time. Just as He can now.

He's hardly moving, fighting for consciousness. I can barely hear the whisper that leaves His lips. "Rumpelstiltskin … you belong … to yourself."

I sense that same break as before, like the world itself has cracked. I'm cold and weak and, oh heavens, I'm *free*.

Strong arms sweep me up and carry me on a slow run through the forest. My human body reminds me it hasn't slept in days. I close my eyes against the chest of the miller's son and rest as I haven't done in years.

A week later, we're settled in a cottage in the sparsely inhabited foothills at the edge of a range of craggy mountains. Cole bought it outright—the iron spindle wasn't the only thing in his pocket when he followed my straw arrows to the clearing. He'd stolen a skein of golden thread too.

For the first time in a week, we're alone. Before leaving the castle, Cole asked the princess to free his father from the dungeon. The miller has been traveling with us as we flee the king, and now he's sleeping in one of the cottage's bedrooms. Cole and I are sitting on a bench on the back porch, and I'm awkwardly trying to think of a way to offer to find my own home now that we're safe. It's a tricky thing, considering I have no money.

I turn to Cole and say, "I hated watching you kiss the princess." My eyes widen, and my cheeks go hot, because that is most definitely not what I planned to tell him.

The lantern a few feet away illuminates his smile, and a low laugh leaves his chest. "Watching you kiss that damn Fae about killed me."

It's my turn to laugh. "Sorry about that."

His smile disappears, and his eyes drop to my lips. He opens his mouth, but I know what he's going to ask, so I speak first.

"Yes, Cole. Yes, you may——"

His lips crush mine. I'm lost—in the heat of his touch and the taste of his mouth. In his fingers gripping my hair and sliding along my skin. In the assurance that he'll only ever take what I choose to give.

Then I whisper his name, and he whispers mine.

And I'm found.

~

I hope you enjoyed *Straw into Gold*!

Beauty and Deceit is my newest retelling. It's *Beauty and the Beast* meets *The Bachelor/The Selection*, and it's a fast-paced, fun story with Fae, action, romance, and just a hint of steam!

Grab your ebook, paperback, or audiobook copy now!

Thank you for reading *Straw into Gold*! Reviews make a *huge* difference to authors and readers. Will you write a short review on Goodreads or your retailer of choice? I can't tell you how much I'd appreciate it.

Do you love romantic fantasy stories featuring Fae characters? You can read *Faerie Flight*, a romantic-fantasy short story, for free as one of my Email Insiders!

Go to CarolBethAnderson.com to get *Faerie Flight* or free.

ABOUT THE AUTHOR

Carol Beth Anderson is an author and professional audio-book narrator who grew up in Arizona and now lives in Leander, TX, outside Austin. Beth has a husband, two kids, and a miniature schnauzer. Besides writing, she loves baking sourdough bread, knitting, and reading lots and lots of books.

facebook.com/carolbethanderson

twitter.com/CBethAnderson

instagram.com/CBethAnderson

bookbub.com/profile/carol-beth-anderson

goodreads.com/carolbethanderson

amazon.com/author/carolbethanderson

tiktok.com/@cbethanderson